Top to Toe Counting

Contents

written by Pam Holden

I can count all the
parts of my body.

I have one head
with one neck.

I have one face with one nose and two ears.

My face has one chin and two cheeks.

I have two eyebrows over my two eyes.

My eyes have lots and lots of eyelashes.

I have one mouth with two lips and one tongue.

I have one big smile with lots of teeth.

I have two shoulders and two arms.

My arms have two
wrists and two elbows.

I have two hands
with ten fingers.

Two of my fingers
are thumbs.

I have two legs with two knees and two ankles.

My two feet have ten toes.

I can't count all the hairs on my head!